CAMILLA, CARTOGRAPHER

by **Julie Dillemuth, PhD**
illustrated by **Laura Wood**

Magination Press • Washington, DC • American Psychological Association

For TH and the wild boars of the Grunewald, and for Clara and Luisa, who love maps as much as their mama does —*JD*

To you, if you feel lost —*LW*

 Order books here: www.apa.org/pubs/magination or 1-800-374-2721

Book design by Gwen Grafft
Printed by Phoenix Color Corporation, Hagerstown, MD

Library of Congress Cataloging-in-Publication Data
Names: Dillemuth, Julie, author. | Wood, Laura, 1985- illustrator. Title: Camilla, cartographer / by Julie Dillemuth ; illustrated by Laura Wood.
Description: Washington, DC : Magination Press, an imprint of the American Psychological Association, [2019] | Summary: When a heavy snowfall leads Camilla, a boar, and her porcupine friend, Parsley, into uncharted territory, Camilla's love of maps and cartography helps them find the path to the creek.
Identifiers: LCCN 2018030575 | ISBN 9781433830334 (hardcover) | ISBN 1433830337 (hardcover)
Subjects: | CYAC: Maps—Fiction. | Cartography—Fiction. | Snow—Fiction. | Boars—Fiction. | Porcupines—Fiction.
Classification: LCC PZ7.1.D56 Cam 2019 | DDC [E]—dc23
LC record available at https://lccn.loc.gov/2018030575

Manufactured in the United States of America
10 9 8 7 6 5 4 3 2 1

When the whirling, swirling snow dusted over the windows and silenced the forest outside, Camilla knew what she wanted to do. She arranged three boxes in front of the fire, and opened her favorite collection.

So many maps! Old ones on crisping paper with golden-brown edges.
Glossy, vibrant, new ones left behind by summertime hikers.

She had mini maps and skinny maps,
furled maps and folded maps.
She even had maps of imaginary places.

Then Camilla took out the most fascinating one of all: an ancient map of her own forest, fragile and faded and scented with time. Her whiskers quivered, her snout shivered.

"What was it like to explore, and to make the first paths?" she whispered. "By now, everything has been explored and mapped." Her hoof traced the outlines of buildings and roads. "It was so different here, long ago. These paths have been lost and forgotten."

Outside, the snow piled higher and deeper.

The next morning, Camilla awoke to a
thump-thump-thump on the window.
“There’s too much snow!” said her neighbor, Parsley.
“I can’t find the path to the creek.”

“I’ll help,” Camilla said.

They trammeled and tamped and trudged.
Shuffled, snuffled, and swooshed.

Until they hit a door.

"We're back at my house!"

Parsley snorted. "How will we get anywhere? This snow could take days to melt!"

Camilla dashed inside and riffled through a box.
"We have this!" She held up a hiker's map of the forest.

They set out again.

But the snow covered everything — familiar boulders, ruins, signposts, every forest path. Camilla tried to match up something, anything, to the map. But it was no use.

"It's like everything we know is gone!" Parsley's words huffed out in cloud-puffs. "We're lost, and we haven't even left home."

Camilla held very still. Her whiskers quivered. Her snout shivered. "This," she said, "is uncharted territory."

“What’s that?” Parsley asked.

“A new land!” Camilla said.
“Unexplored, and unmapped!”
She flew inside for supplies.

"You're in charge of this," she said, handing Parsley a compass.
"Are we still trying to find the path?" Parsley asked.
Camilla leaned in close. "We get to make new paths. Our own paths."

They scrabbled, scraped,
and stomped.

"We know the creek is east,
same as the morning sun."

"Then we'd better change course,
because we're heading southeast!"

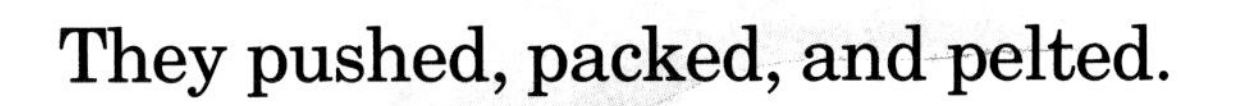

They pushed, packed, and pelted.

Mulled, measured,
and marked.

"Uh oh."

"Ta-da!" Camilla said when they reached the creek. "Now, we map."

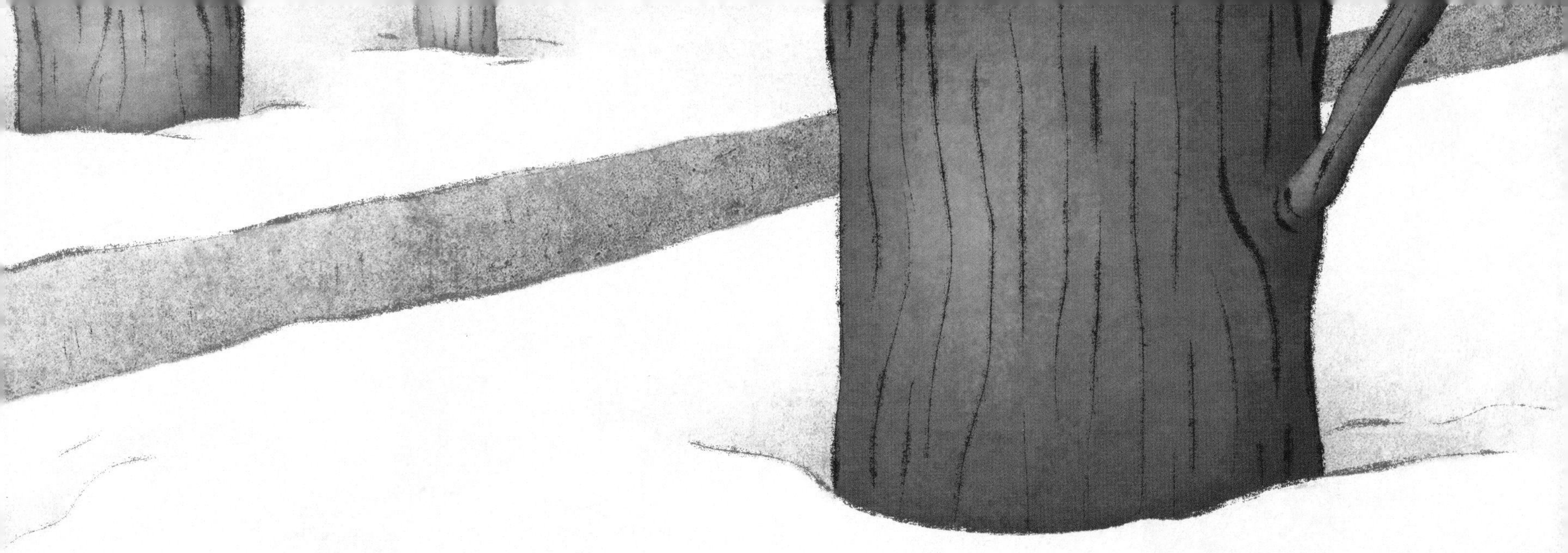

She organized her supplies and began to draw: her house, the creek, the paths she and Parsley had cleared. The tallest trees and towers that poked up out of the snow. In the bottom corner she sketched a compass rose in the shape of a snowflake. Across the top of the map she wrote a title in a curly flourish. And she signed it:

Camilla, Cartographer

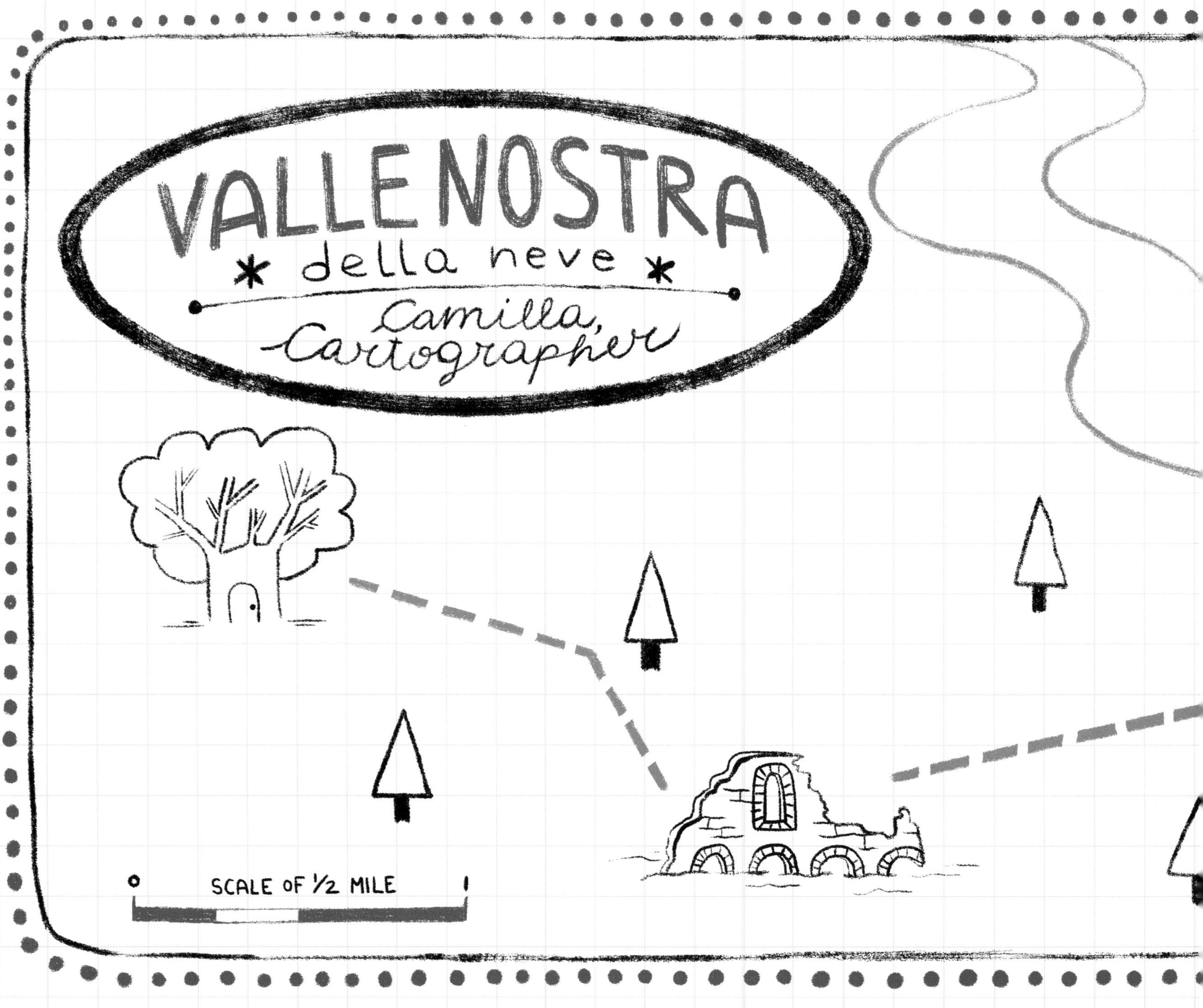

VALLE NOSTRA
* della neve *
Camilla, Cartographer

SCALE OF ½ MILE

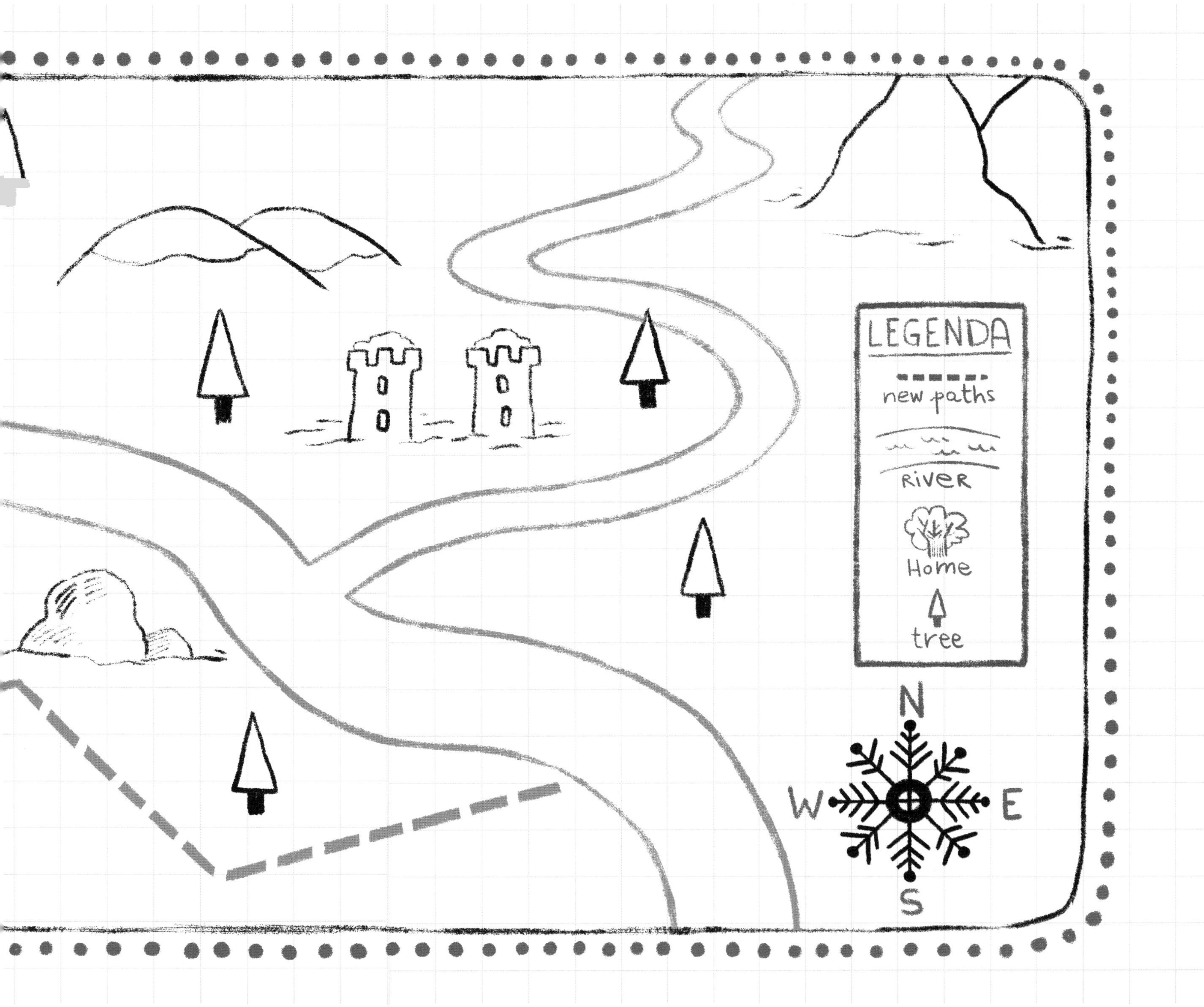
LEGENDA
new paths
River
Home
tree
N
W
E
S

"There's more to explore," Parsley said. "Before the snow melts."
Camilla froze. "When it melts! Our paths will be lost and forgotten." She hugged her map and squeezed her eyes shut.

The snow made the silence especially quiet.

She opened her eyes.
“Our paths will
always be here,
on this map.”

Back home, Camilla placed her new map next to the fragile and faded one. She traced the paths with a hoof.

"Not everything has already been mapped."

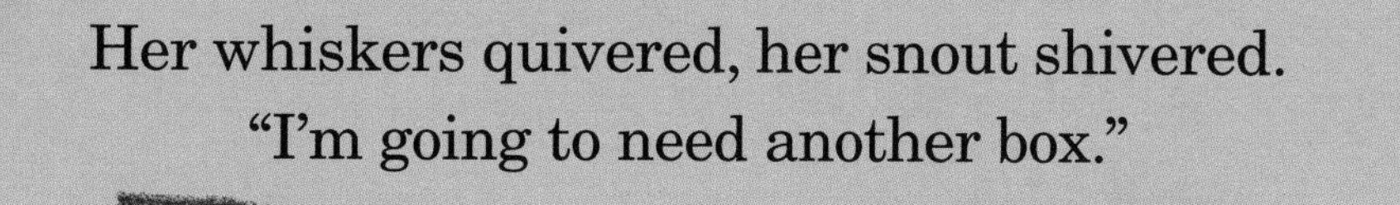

Her whiskers quivered, her snout shivered.
"I'm going to need another box."

NOTE TO PARENTS AND CAREGIVERS

In this book, Camilla is fascinated by maps of all kinds, especially a historical map of her own forest that shows how different the roads and buildings were long ago. She's under the false impression that everything has already been explored and mapped, but by the end of the story, after snow transforms the landscape, she realizes that she can still make new discoveries, forge her own paths, and document her activities in maps. This story is a great starting point for encouraging both spatial thinking skills and your child's curiosity about exploring and discovering new adventures.

Spatial Thinking Skills

"Spatial thinking" refers to how we understand the world around us and use concepts of space for problem solving. We rely on spatial thinking skills in everyday life, and these skills are important for math and science learning as children progress through school. In daily life, when we pack a backpack so that everything fits, or use words like "on," "under," or "next to," which describe how things are related in space, we're thinking spatially. More challenging spatial tasks include things like using a small, flat map in the large, 3D landscape; interpreting a graph or chart; or imagining and mentally rotating objects such as the movements of the earth, moon, and sun during an eclipse.

Spatial thinking skills are important to develop from an early age, and like any skill, it takes practice—the more, the better! Spatial thinking elements in *Camilla, Cartographer* include orienting and navigating with a compass, drawing maps, and exploring outdoors. Read on to learn more about these topics and get ideas for activities to do with your child.

Orienting and Navigating With a Compass

A compass tells you where the cardinal directions north, south, east, and west are, in the palm of your hand. Camilla's map is no use when the entire landscape is covered with snow, but she can find her way with a compass. She and Parsley already know the general direction of the creek, so by using the compass to set a course, they can continue in one direction and not end up digging in a circle again. Without a compass, since they can't see over the snow, it's easy to lose orientation and veer off course. When they encounter an obstacle and change direction, the compass helps them keep track of changes they make to their course. Camilla also keeps track of the distances of all the path segments, so that she can make her map once they find the creek.

Activity: Help your child understand the cardinal directions, north, south, east, and west. A compass points north because the magnetized needle in it is attracted to the earth's magnetic north pole. Don't have a compass? You can find an inexpensive one at an outdoors store or a toy store. Or make your own, by rubbing a needle with a magnet to magnetize it, then floating it in water so it can rotate freely (there are many tutorials for this online!).

Unless you're in an epic snowstorm like Camilla and Parsley, in a real-life situation you are more likely to use a compass along with a map. From the map, you can determine your destination and the direction in which it lies, and then you can use the compass to stay on course as you navigate there. Choose an appropriate destination with your child, such as a place in a park, or from your house to school or the library, and let your child take the lead in navigating you there. Mistakes along the way are okay! For more information, search the internet for "map and compass" and you will find many tutorials and detailed instructions.

Map Making

A cartographer is someone who makes maps, who simplifies the vast, wide, complex world onto a piece of paper or a computer screen through a combination of science and art. Maps help us learn about the world, from the area we see around us to places we've never been. As drawings that show relationships of things in space, they let us compare information about places, across space or time. Involving your child in reading, making, and using maps helps them develop their spatial thinking skills, and can inspire them to explore and discover.

Activity: Sketch a map in the typical "north up" orientation. Scientists and professional cartographers make careful measurements for an accurate map, but for a fun activity like this we can keep it simple. Pick a large area with interesting features, such as a park or playground. Show your child how to use a compass to orient yourselves facing north. Choose a place to sit so you have a good view, facing north, of the area you're going to map. In one corner of a sheet of paper, have your child draw a compass rose (simple crossed lines or arrows will do) and consult the compass to label N, S, E, and W. Then your child can start drawing the map—paths, trees, grass, playground equipment, etc. Talk about the cardinal directions. Notice in which direction the sun is, and where shadows are pointing. You can have fun with your map by drawing in a route for the other person to follow, or hiding an object for the other person to find and giving a hint by pointing to where it is on the map. Your child may have other ideas about how to use the map—follow their lead!

Exploration and Discovery

Before the snowstorm, Camilla thinks there is nothing new left to explore. Broadening this idea, it's important for kids to realize that even though it may seem like everything has already been discovered and that grown-ups have all the answers, there is still so much we don't know. Remind kids that there are many more discoveries yet to be made, and that they can investigate questions and make discoveries themselves, right now and when they are grown up. Encourage them to be curious and ask questions.

Activity: Find historical maps of a place that interests you and your child, and compare what is the same then as now, and what is different. You can search the internet for historical maps, or start at a website such as OldMapsOnline (www.oldmapsonline.org), where you can choose maps from the past to overlay onto a current map. What types of things stay the same over time? What changes?

Activity: Go exploring! The American Academy of Pediatrics' 2018 clinical report, *The Power of Play*, calls for increased play time for children, especially unstructured free play. Outdoor play time is essential, and exploring real-world environments develops and tests important spatial skills. Let Camilla and Parsley be your inspiration: While they have a real goal to find the creek, they also create their own world by pretending they are in a new, unexplored place. Get outside, stand back, and watch your child's imagination take over.

On Accepting Change

When Camilla realizes her new paths are going to go away when the snow melts, she is distraught, until she takes comfort that her map will forever preserve them. It's hard for all of us, especially kids, to let go and to accept change. Acknowledge those feelings. Sometimes it helps to take a photo or make a drawing, to help keep a memory of something before it goes away, to make letting go a little easier.

Have fun with these activities, and think of your own to help you and your child practice spatial thinking! Get into a habit of incorporating spatial thinking challenges into your child's daily routine: Let them figure out how to fit everything in their backpack, or quiz them on the way to school about which direction you're heading and where the sun is. Model the attitude that a challenge is an interesting problem to figure out. You will be helping to set your child up for success with important life and education skills.

About the Author

Julie Dillemuth, PhD, scrabbled through snow as a kid, pored over old maps as an archaeology major in college, and learned to map with a compass before the world revolved around GPS. She has a PhD in geography with an emphasis in cognitive science, and writes children's books in Santa Barbara, California, where the west coast faces south. Visit juliedillemuth.com.

About the Illustrator

Laura Wood is an independent illustrator currently based in Milan, Italy. Her work can be found in textbooks, advertising campaigns, digital apps, and editorial publications. But mostly she likes to illustrate picture books and bring stories to life. Her favorite things include coffee, dancing, and visiting new places. She is proudly represented by the lovely people at Good Illustration Agency. Visit laurawoodillustration.com.

About Magination Press

Magination Press is the children's book imprint of the American Psychological Association. Through APA's publications, the association shares with the world mental health expertise and psychological knowledge. Magination Press books reach young readers and their parents and caregivers to make navigating life's challenges a little easier. It's the combined power of psychology and literature that makes a Magination Press book special. Visit maginationpress.org.